NICK JR The BACKYARDIGANS

Riding the Range

adapted by Justin Spelvin
based on the original teleplay by McPaul Smith
illustrated by The Artifact Group

SIMON SPOTLIGHT / NICK JR.
New York   London   Toronto   Sydney

Based on the TV series *Nick Jr. The Backyardigans*™ as seen on Nick Jr.®

SIMON SPOTLIGHT
An imprint of Simon & Schuster Children's Publishing Division
1230 Avenue of the Americas, New York, New York 10020
© 2006 Viacom International Inc.
Manufactured in the United States of America
First Edition
2 4 6 8 10 9 7 5 3 1
Library of Congress Cataloging-in-Publication Data
Spelvin, Justin.
Riding the range / adapted by Justin Spelvin; based on the original teleplay by McPaul Smith.—1st ed.
p. cm.—(Ready-to-read)
"Based on the TV series Nick Jr. Backyardigans created by Janice Burgess as seen on Nick Jr."
ISBN-13: 978-1-4169-1304-7
ISBN-10: 1-4169-1304-1
I.Smith, McPaul. II.Backyardigans (Television program) III.Title. IV.Series.
PZ7.S74735Rid 2006   [E]--dc22   2005020696

"Yeehaw! I am a cowboy!"

says . "Whose is this?"

TYRONE   ROPE

Cowboy 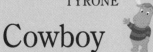 sets out

TYRONE

to find the 's owner.

ROPE

"Hey! My 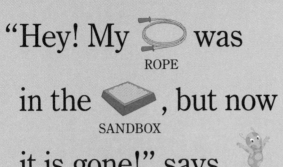 was
ROPE

in the 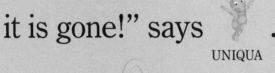, but now
SANDBOX

it is gone!" says  .
UNIQUA

"Look!"  says. " !"

PABLO   FOOTPRINTS

"Cowboy made these

BOOTS

!" says .

FOOTPRINTS   TASHA

"There is a bandit

on the loose," says .

PABLO

"We need to find him!"

 ,  , and

PABLO   TASHA   UNIQUA

put on their  and climb

HATS

on to their  .

HORSES

"The  go into that
canyon,"  says.

TRACKS

PABLO

"It is dark," says  .

TASHA

 ,  , and  ride

PABLO   TASHA   UNIQUA

into the canyon.

Soon they are lost!

"How do we get out?"

asks  .

TASHA

"The walls are too tall,"

says.

UNIQUA

Then someone calls out,

"Howdy, down there!"

It is Cowboy !
TYRONE

"When your  sees an ,"
HORSE   APPLE

says   , "it will climb out.
TYRONE

 love !" takes
HORSES   APPLES   TYRONE

an from his .
APPLE   BAG

The  climb toward the ● !

HORSES   APPLE

● , ● , and ● thank

PABLO   TASHA   UNIQUA

● for his help.

TYRONE

"It is time to sleep,"

says.

TASHA

The next day  TYRONE wakes up

and gets on his  HORSE .

"I will let the others sleep,"

says  TYRONE .

As rides away,

TYRONE

 fall from his 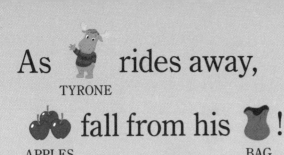!

APPLES   BAG

The other  are hungry,

HORSES

so they follow the !

APPLES

, , and  wake up.

PABLO   TASHA   UNIQUA

 and the  are gone!

TYRONE   HORSES

"The bandit took them!"

says .

PABLO

 follows the  .

PABLO   TRACKS

 and  follow  .

UNIQUA   TASHA   PABLO

"The bandit must be in

that !" says.
      CABIN   PABLO

, , and

tiptoe to the ▪ .
                         DOOR

PABLO   TASHA   UNIQUA

Then they rush

into the !
CABIN

"Howdy!" says .

 sees 's lasso.

"That is my 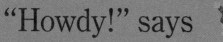 !"

TYRONE

UNIQUA   TYRONE

JUMP ROPE

"I was looking for the owner," says .

TYRONE

 gives the 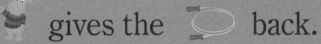 back.

TYRONE   JUMP ROPE

Then 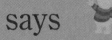 tummy rumbles.

UNIQUA'S

"We can go to my
HOUSE

for 🍪," 🐧 says.
COOKIES   PABLO

"That is good," says 🐂.
TYRONE

"I am all out of 🍎!"
APPLES